HI, CAT!

EZRA JACK KEATS

COLLIER BOOKS
DIVISION OF MACMILLAN PUBLISHING CO., INC.
New York

Copyright © 1970 Ezra Jack Keats. All rights reserved. No part of this book may be reproduced or transmitted in any form or by any means, electronic or mechanical, including photocopying, recording or by any information storage and retrieval system, without permission in writing from the Publisher. Macmillan Publishing Co., Inc., 866 Third Avenue, New York, N.Y. 10022.
Collier Macmillan Canada, Inc. Library of Congress Catalog Card Number: 71-102968. *Hi, Cat!* is published in a hardcover edition by Macmillan Publishing Co., Inc. Printed in the United States of America. First Collier Books Edition 1972. ISBN 0-02-044120-7   10 9 8 7

For David Hautzig

On his way to meet Peter,
Archie saw someone new on the block.

"Hi, cat," he said as he walked by.

He looked at his reflection in a store window.

Peter was waiting at the corner.
"Make way for your ol' gran'pa,"
Archie said in a shaky voice.
He looked Peter up and down.
"My, my, Peter, how you've grown!"

"Why, gran'pa," Peter said.

"It's good to see you."

"Hello, my children," Archie croaked.

"Hi, gran'pa!" Susy giggled.

Willie was so happy to see Archie
he ran over and licked his face.
Archie tasted delicious!
Willie licked and licked and licked.

"No respect for old age!"

Archie whispered something to Peter and ran off.
"Stick around, folks," Peter called.
"We have a surprise for you."

When Archie got back,
he and Peter worked
while everyone waited.

"OK!" Peter announced.
"Make way for Mister Big Face!"
A big paper bag appeared.
Then a tongue stuck out of one of the eyes!

A hand came out of an ear
and motioned everyone to move closer.
They all obeyed.

Suddenly the bag began to shake.

It shook harder, and harder, and—

MEEOOW!

People started to leave.

"Wait—wait—the show'll go on!
See the tallest dog in the world
take a walk!" Archie shouted.

"Some show, gran'pa!"
"Some tall dog!"
"Who ate your mustache, gran'pa?"
Everyone walked away, laughing.
Soon no one was left except Archie, Peter,
Willie and the torn paper bag.

"It would have been great
   if it wasn't for that crazy cat," said Peter
   as they walked home.
"Mmmm," said Archie. "He sure stuck around."

". . . and all I said was 'Hi, cat,' " said Archie,
  finishing his story.
"You're well rid of a cat like that,"
  said his mother.
  Archie thought for a while.
"You know what, Ma?" he said.
"I think that cat just kinda liked me!"

a straw
me then that
br

ago, whe
ent/o